WHEN
HUMAN HEADS
WERE
FOOTBALLS

WHEN HUMAN HEADS WERE FOOTBALLS

- -

Surprising Stories of How Sports Began

By Don L. Wulffson
Illustrated by Mike Dietz

Aladdin Paperbacks

**In Memory of My Father,
Charles R. Wulffsohn**

Photograph on p. 7 courtesy of Reuters/Corbis-Bettman
Photograph on p. 12 courtesy of the Associated Press/Providence Journal-Bulletin
Photographs on pp. 22-23 courtesy of the Baseball Hall of Fame Library, Cooperstown, NY
Photograph on p. 26 courtesy of the Associated Press
Photographs on pp. 40, 43 courtesy of UPI/Corbis-Bettman
Photograph on p. 47 courtesy of Agence France Presse/Corbis Bettman

First Aladdin Paperbacks edition August 1998

Aladdin Paperbacks
An imprint of Simon & Schuster Children's Publishing Division
1230 Avenue of the Americas
New York, NY 10020

Library of Congress Cataloging-in-Publication Data
Wulffson, Don L.
When human heads were footballs :
surprising stories of how sports began / by Don L. Wulffson.
p.   cm.
Summary: Recounts a variety of unusual stories
behind the invention of such sports as
football, basketball, and baseball.
ISBN 0-689-81959-5 (pbk.)
1. Sports—History—Juvenile literature.
2. Sports—Humor—Juvenile literature. [1. Sports—History.] I. Title.
GV571.W86   1998
796'.09—dc21   97-52166
CIP   AC

TABLE OF CONTENTS

INTRODUCTION

- -

What sport almost ended up being called boxball? Which one was once played with a dried, inflated cow bladder? And which one started out as a fortune-telling ritual, and ended up, centuries later, being named after an Englishman's house?

When Human Heads Were Footballs answers these questions and a great many more. It tells the stories of how some of our most popular sports came to be. The stories are often amusing, usually surprising, and some-times just plain weird!

One

FOOTBALL

A BLOODY WONDERFUL GAME!

"Head Start"

Imagine using a human head as a football! Sounds pretty gross, but believe it or not, that's the way football began. One day in the eighth century, several ships loaded with Vikings showed up on the shores of England. Hurling spears, firing arrows, and waving swords overhead, the Vikings stormed ashore to conquer jolly old England.

The Vikings got trounced. And their leader got captured. The English whacked off his head. Then, for fun, they kicked the head around and made a real game of it. Exactly what the rules of this first football game were, nobody knows. And nobody knows who won. Regardless, a new sport had begun.

Bladder Ball!

But the English didn't fight a battle every day, so there wasn't always a head to kick around. Enthusiasts of the sport needed something else to use as a ball, and what they came up with was almost as gross as a human head. They cut the bladder out of a dead cow, let it dry in the sun, and then blew it up and tied it off. That's why the rubber, air-filled bag inside a football is still called a "bladder" to this day.

Cow bladders had an annoying tendency to pop. They just couldn't take all that kicking around. To prevent this, people began covering the bladders with animal skin. Cowhide, deerskin, and goat hide were all given a try. But pigskin turned out to work the best. In fact it's still often used, and you guessed it: that's why a football today is referred to as a "pigskin."

Broken Bones and Busted Homes!

"Townball"—that's what football was called during the Middle Ages. Everybody got into the act: Gertrude the baker, Purvis the cook, Bruno the blacksmith, and anybody else who wanted to play was welcome—if they didn't mind getting smashed up a bit. You see, townball was a wild, violent free-for-all. Punching, gouging, and stomping were all legal.

As the name townball implies, the main street of the town was the field, with the goal being to somehow get the pigskin to the opponent's end of town. Teams were roughly equal in number, with each team consisting of about 200 screaming men, women, and children. Often, a single game would last an entire day. When it was over, the town was in a shambles, and the injured—and sometimes dead—players were hauled away.

In time, local authorities got fed up with townball, and they made it illegal. "You're destroying the town, you fools!" they declared. "If you want to kill yourselves, that's your business. But go play your game out in a field where you won't smash up the town!"

And that's exactly what the players did. They took their pigskin and went out to a level, grassy area. Once there, they set up boundaries and goal lines. The number of players was reduced. The total wasn't standardized, but the two teams had to be equal.

The Runaround at Rugby School

The game played in those early days was more like soccer than American football. The ball could be kicked or hit with any part of the body, but players were not allowed to run with the ball or throw it.

This all changed at a match played at Rugby, a private boys' school in Warwickshire, England, in 1823. During the game, a kid named William Ellis got super frustrated. Again and again he missed the bouncing ball when he tried to kick it. In a moment of rage, he picked up the ball and raced with it down the field.

"Ellis, you numbskull!" the coach screamed. "Blimey, boy! Ya can't be runnin' with the ball! Go sit on the bench!"

Though his coach was furious at him for breaking the rules, and a lot of the

Ellis is a daffy bloke!

I thought what he did was bloody wonderful!

Running with the ball would be a most excellent innovation!

other kids laughed at him, what Ellis had done stirred the imagination of many of the players.

And that's how a new type of game came into being—a game in which players could run with the ball. People started calling the sport "rugby," after the school where William Ellis, in a moment of frustration, had given it its start.

In the U.S.—A Smashing Success

Early in the nineteenth century, football made its way across the Atlantic to the United States. At first it was sort of a mix of rugby and soccer. Kicking was still most important. A field goal scored five points. A safety counted for one point. Originally, running into the end zone and "touching the ball down" (a touchdown) was good for only two points. In 1883 the value of a touchdown was changed to four points; in 1897 it was upped to five points; in 1912 the value increased to six points, where it remains today.

> In pro football, how many yards was the longest field goal ever kicked?
>
> A) 52 yards
> B) 78 yards
> C) 63 yards
>
> (see below for the answer)

Little by little, over the next hundred years an all-American brand of football evolved. First off, it was in America that the ball was given its egg-like shape, as compared to the much rounder rugby ball. Then the length of the field was changed, from 110 yards to 100. Next, the game was divided into two halves, with a rest period in between. Originally, each half was forty-five minutes. That made the game kind of long, so the halves were changed to only 30 minutes, as today.

4

Saving Heads

In the early days of football the players did not wear helmets. To protect them-selves, footballers took to wearing their hair long. Sometimes they even tied their hair up in buns on top of their heads. Back then, there was also no padding—no protection for legs, hips, and shoulders. American football players in those days got really messed up, even more so than players today.

Finally, enough was enough. Tired of getting bruised and battered, toward the end of the nineteenth century some players started wearing homemade leather helmets and pads. At first, they were laughed at and heckled. The other players called them sissies . . . until they finally wised up and started wearing them, too.

Anything Goes!

At about this time, the idea of a line of scrimmage was established. But the players didn't exactly line up like they do today. The linemen didn't crouch in a three-point stance. Instead, they just stood face-to-face! When the ball was snapped, the linemen immediately started punching, tackling, and wrestling each other.

But linemen tearing into each other like that wasn't the strangest part of early football. Today it's illegal, but back then the players were allowed to pick up the guy carrying the ball and run with him! Sometimes, enemy tacklers would be clinging to the ball carrier's legs, trying to hold him back, while several of his teammates would be pulling him in the opposite direction toward the goal line. It's a wonder the poor guy wasn't ripped in half!

Get Down!

A team was allowed only three downs in those days to make a first down. But that wasn't as tough as it sounds. You see, back then, a team was only required to gain five yards for a new set of downs. Today, of course, a team is given four downs, but it has to go ten yards.

A Number of No-Shows

Originally, the number of players on each team was fifteen, as in rugby. One day the number simply *had* to be changed. The year was 1874. Teams from Cambridge University and McGill University agreed to meet for a football game. But at the last minute, four members of the McGill squad were unable to make the trip. The only thing that could be done was to change the number of players on each team to eleven. It's been eleven ever since.

True or False?

Three women have played in the NFL.

Air America!

Though the number of players went down, another number was soon going up—yards gained on average by a team. It's all because of the forward pass, which was made legal in 1906. At first, few teams bothered using it. But then one day in 1913, Notre Dame played Army (the United States Military Academy at West Point). The Army players were big, tough, and bruising. Notre Dame's players were little pipsqueaks by comparison. In desperation, Notre Dame resorted to the forward pass—and whipped Army, 35–13. After seeing what an amazing weapon the passing game could be, teams all over the country started using it. Probably more than anything else, it was the forward pass that made football into one of the most exciting and most uniquely American sports in the world today.

Two

BOWLING
FROM CHURCHYARD TO ALLEYWAY

- -

Get the Devil!

It's the third century. You're in Germany . . . in a church, to be exact. Prayers are said. Hymns are sung. A sermon is given. And now it's time for the last part of the service. Now everybody has to go bowling!

Incredibly, that's how the sport began. It started out as part of early Christian religious ceremonies in Germany. After the morning service, people went out into the churchyard. There, a single wooden pin, a little larger than those used today, was set up. The pin was supposed to represent the devil. Everybody got in line. Then, one after another, churchgoers rolled or threw a stone about the size of a baseball at the pin. If you hit the pin and knocked it over it didn't mean you were a good shot; it meant you were a good Christian. You'd just knocked the devil out of your life. As for those who missed . . . well, they had to come back next Sunday and try to prove themselves again.

The priests also bowled. In fact, they did a lot to make bowling more like the sport we know today. They didn't bowl using just one pin; a group of pins was set up together, as many pins as there were participants. With all those pins to knock over, the priests soon realized that a small stone wasn't going to do the trick. They began using a bigger one; one about the size of a modern bowling ball. The winner—and best Christian—was the person who knocked down the most pins, or devils.

After All, It's Just a Game!

Two centuries passed. And during this time, little by little, people began to like bowling for its own sake. Everyone—including the priests—stopped thinking of it as a religious ceremony. Instead, they saw it for what it really was—something that was good exercise and fun to do. They saw it as a sport.

House Rules

Sometimes people took the sport indoors, and bowled in their houses. The furnishings—all the chairs and tables and rugs—were shoved aside. Then out came the bowling equipment. So the house and floor wouldn't get wrecked, players used a solid rubber bowling ball. The pins were specially-shaped and were a little smaller than the ones previously used in churches.

The Alley Way

For outdoor bowling, people played on lawns, at least at first. The problem with grass, however, was that it slowed the ball down too much. (The grass

was just too long—for the simple reason the lawn mower hadn't been invented yet!) So people did a lot of experimenting and finally decided on alleys of hardened clay, which provided a fast, smooth surface. For outdoor bowling, a ball of iron or solid wood was used.

Today, what's the maximum weight allowed for a bowling ball?

From Holy to Holey

For a long time, the ball had to be palmed—that is, rolled off the end of the hand. Then one day in the fourteenth century, somebody came up with the bright idea of drilling finger holes in the ball. At first just two holes were drilled, one for the thumb and one for the middle finger. Then came the three-hole ball, like those we use today.

Pinning Down the Number

People had a lot of trouble agreeing on how many pins should be used in bowling. During the Middle Ages, people all over Europe bowled. But the number of pins varied from place to place. You might go to one town and find the people using five pins. Go to another town, and the alleys would be set up with seventeen! A few miles away the people might insist there should be just one pin, like in the "good old days."

Not until the sixteenth century did people finally agree on a number, and that was because of a man named Martin Luther. Martin Luther was a famous Protestant reformer who also happened to like bowling. After fiddling around with different numbers and setups, he came to the conclusion that nine was best, with the pins set up in a boxlike shape in three rows of three pins each. "If that's the way the Reverend Luther does it, then that's the way it should be done," said Lutherans, the cleric's followers. And pretty soon other people, following their example, were using nine pins, too.

To America...and around the Law

No one knows exactly when the game of "ninepins," as it was called, first arrived in America. All that's known is sometime in the eighteenth century a ship arrived from Holland, and one of the male passengers had a bowling ball and bowling pins with him.

In America, ninepins became a gambling game and was usually played in places where a lot of seedy characters—crooks, bums, thieves—hung out. Because of this, ninepins was outlawed. Getting around the law, however, wasn't hard at all. The players just added one more pin. And because the law said that ninepins was illegal but didn't say anything about *tenpins*, there was nothing the cops could do. And that is why to this day, the game of bowling is played with ten pins.

Today, how many strikes are in a perfect game of bowling?

Three

TENNIS
THE OVER-AND-OVER INVENTED GAME

Mary's Story

It was March 20, 1874. Mary Outerbridge, a young American girl, was returning to her home in New York from a vacation in Bermuda. With her she had some foreign-looking sports equipment—wacky rackets, felt-covered balls, and some kind of newfangled net. On Bermuda, Mary had learned a great new sport. In her yard at home, Mary set up the equipment. Her girlfriends played the game with her—but very reluctantly. They were afraid they'd seem "unladylike"! But little by little,

I am not sure it is ladylike to go racing and leaping in pursuit of a flying or bouncing ball.

Is it 'unladylike' to have fun?

the girls quit worrying about being "ladylike" and really started to get into the game.

Now and then, Mary's two brothers watched from the sidelines. One day they decided to try the game themselves. The two were having a good time . . . until some of their buddies saw them and started laughing and making fun of them for playing a "girls' game."

The Outerbridge brothers challenged the other guys to play. Taking up the dare as though it was a big joke, the other boys quickly found out how much skill, speed, and toughness tennis takes.

Soon both boys and girls, and men and women, were playing tennis in the New York area. And from there the game quickly spread across the country.

A Major Breakthrough—A Minor Problem

Mary Outerbridge introduced the sport to the United States, but she didn't invent it. Major Walter C. Wingfield, a British Army officer, didn't invent it, either. But he thought he did. This is what happened. One day in 1873 Wingfield was reading about life in ancient Greece and stumbled upon a description of a sport called *Spharistike*. In *Spharistike* players used the palms of their hands to whack a ball back and forth over a net. Inspired, Wingfield decided to create his own, modern version of the game.

Within a few days, Wingfield came up with all the rules and equipment for his "new" game. Like the Greeks, he called it *Spharistike*, which means "let's play!" But in Wingfield's game, a racket, instead of an open hand, was used to hit the ball. And the balls were made of solid rubber rather than wound-up leather. As for the court, Wingfield's was shaped like an hourglass, narrower at the net than in the backcourt area. The net was hung high, as in badminton, a game Wingfield had learned in India. Additional nets, called "side curtains," also were hung.

Wingfield's friends and relatives played the game and loved it. They thought everything about it was great—except the side curtains. No one—including Wingfield—was sure what their purpose was, and the silly things came down.

Overall, Wingfield was very pleased with himself and extremely excited about the future of the game. If friends and family took to it so readily, he figured, so would thousands of people! And he could patent his invention and make millions!

But shortly after going to the patent office, Wingfield's bubble burst. A patent was issued to him for *Spharistike*. But after receiving it, Wingfield learned he had invented a game that was new *to him* but, known by different names, was not new to others. It had *already been invented*—by the French, centuries before—and had long been a popular pastime, not only in many European countries, but even in some parts of England!

Though he was upset about all this, Wingfield did not lose his enthusiasm for the sport. In the following years he did much to standardize its rules and spread its popularity—first throughout England, then to its colonies. One of these colonies was Bermuda, where Mary Outerbridge first played the game.

> *In France, for a time, playing tennis was a craze among Christian monks. In fact, they liked it so much that they started neglecting their religious duties. For this reason, in 1245, the Archbishop of Rouen, France, outlawed them from playing tennis at all.*

The French Try Their Hand

In France, the sport had evolved slowly. Though no one knows for sure, the French, like Wingfield, probably had picked it up from the Greeks. Regardless, by the Middle Ages, French men and women were playing a sport they called *jeu de paum,* which means "the game of the palm." In it, as in *Spharistike,* a ball was hit back and forth over a net using the open hand.

Naturally, whacking a ball with one's hand started to get pretty painful after a while. To soften the blow, players began to wear gloves. The gloves not only guarded against injury, they also enabled the players to hit the ball with greater force.

Little by little, the gloves got bigger and bigger. Made of hardened leather, they looked like paddles.

Whatta Racket!

During the seventeenth century, someone in France came up with a totally new type of "tennis glove." The thing was strange—but also very effective. The palm was rounded inward, with a crisscross mesh of hardened leather strings over it. You can probably guess what happened next. The meshed, oversized glove was taken off the hand and securely attached to a handle. The tennis racket was born!

There's a funny thing about the word "racket." Its history tells a lot about how the item itself came to be invented. Racket comes from the Arabic word *rahat,* meaning "the palm of the hand." Thus, the present name of this piece of sports equipment recalls the fact that it came into being as a substitute for the open hand.

As for the name "tennis," it comes from the French exclamation *tenez.* Loosely translated, *tenez* means "get ready, I'm gonna serve!"

In tennis, the term "love" means "zero, nothing." (For example, the score of a game might be 5–love.) This tennis term came about because the shape of a zero—0—resembles an egg, and in French, l'oeuf means both "egg" and "zero." On English tongues, l'oeuf soon changed into "love."

It's Been a Pleasure to Serve You!

Last but not least, why do we call it a "serve"? As with "racket" and "tennis," the reason is all wound up with the history of the sport. In the England of Wingfield's time, a servant "delivered" the first ball. He not only brought out the ball, he also started the action by tossing it into play! Many, many years have passed since then, but it is from this long-forgotten custom that we get our terms "service" and "serve."

Four

BASEBALL
"STRIKE FOUR, YOU'RE OUT!"

Doubleday Didn't Do It!

Abner Doubleday was a popular kid in Cooperstown, NY. On a summer's day, back in the 1830s, he and his friends often would get together for a game of stickball. Almost always, Abner Graves would be on the same team as Doubleday. The two Abners were best buddies.

When Doubleday grew up, he joined the Union Army. During the Civil War, he fought heroically in several battles. Eventually, he was promoted to general. After the war, he retired from the army and wrote articles for magazines. An honored and respected man, he died in 1893 and was buried in Arlington National Cemetery.

Abner Doubleday was an intelligent and interesting man who did a lot during his lifetime. There is one thing, though, that he did not do. Doubleday did *not* invent baseball.

Many people believe he did. And the reason they do is because of a man named A.G. Spalding. Spalding, a sporting goods manufacturer, was very wealthy and influential, and also highly patriotic. In 1905, he formed a committee to prove that baseball was "invented in America with no connection to any sport previously played in any other nation." Furthermore, he stated that in all probability baseball was the product—the brainchild—"of some ingenious American lad."

After two years of research, Spalding's committee failed to turn up anything to support these claims. Then one day a letter arrived from Abner Graves, Doubleday's boyhood buddy. Graves, now a very frail old man, claimed that Doubleday had not only invented baseball, but had also named it.

Spalding was delighted. He didn't care that Graves did not have a single bit of proof. He didn't care that the letter was probably just the ramblings of an elderly gentleman with fond but fanciful memories of a childhood friend. As far as Spalding was concerned, the letter was the "evidence" he had been looking for, and he proceeded to persuade the committee to go along with him. In 1939, the Baseball Hall of Fame was established at Cooperstown, NY, the hometown of Abner Doubleday, a kid who played baseball but certainly did not invent the game or give it its name.

Actually, what we know today as baseball developed slowly and over a period of hundreds of years. It's an American adaptation of two English games: rounders and cricket.

Rounders: A Quick Run-Down

Rounders was a kids' game. The pitcher was called the "thrower." The batter was called the "striker," and he stood in a shallow hole dug in the ground called the "striker's box." As for the ball, it was made of either solid rubber or tightly wound twine. A stake driven into the ground was the base. Usually there was just one stake; but sometimes there would be two—or even more—to run to. As for the number of players, it didn't matter how many kids were on each team, as long as the teams were more or less equal.

"Okay, let's play ball!" the kids would yell. The thrower went into his windup. Then the pitch. And the striker whacked the ball with a stick . . . and

off he went running. The idea for the runner, of course, was to reach the stake safely. On a good, long hit the runner "rounded" the stake then ran "home" to score. To prevent him from scoring—and to make an out—the fielder could do one of three things. A ball caught on the fly—or after one bounce—was an out. The runner could be tagged out. And last but not least, he could be "plugged." Believe it or not, the ball could be thrown at the runner—and hitting him constituted an out!

Cricket

Cricket is an adult game, and a very complicated one. In it, a "bowler" bounces a hard rubber ball at a stick called a "wicket." Using a large, flat bat, a "batsman" tries to protect the wicket, hit the ball, then run to another wicket (the second of only two used in the game). Scores are made by safely getting from one wicket to the other, or by hitting the ball out of bounds.

English colonists in America played rounders and cricket. Little by little, the two games merged into one, which slowly evolved into the sport of baseball as we know it today.

The Name of the Game

During the eighteenth and nineteenth centuries, the progressively popular game was known by many different names. It was "townball" in Philadelphia and Boston. In New York it was called the "New York game" or "Knickerbocker." Other names for it were "one old cat," "two old cat," and so forth, depending on the number of stakes used.

Stakes aren't fun things to run into. Sick of smashing into them and getting knocked silly, the players decided on a change. The stakes were pulled up and discarded. In their place, flat rocks or sandbags were used. The players called them "bases," since the original meaning of the word refers to something that is "thick, stumpy, and low." Bases really changed the game's action—and also its name. From then on, the name of the game was "baseball!"

> You may have noticed something interesting: both football and baseball were once known as "townball."

Figuring Out the Field

The setup for the playing field in baseball has gone through many changes. In 1842, for example, the field looked like this: ⟶

There were four bases instead of three. The batter had to get to "fourth base" to score. He didn't have to get back to where he started out, back "to home." A "run" in those days was called an "ace," and the first team to score twenty-one aces was the winner.

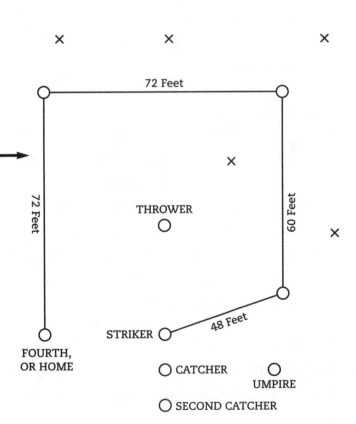

72 Feet

72 Feet

60 Feet

THROWER

STRIKER

48 Feet

FOURTH, OR HOME

CATCHER

UMPIRE

SECOND CATCHER

21

Playing the Field

Players back then were called "scouts," and there were 12 scouts on a team. The extra players were the "infield rover," "outfield rover," and . . . the *second* catcher. It's true! There were always *two* catchers back in the early days of baseball, one behind the other! The reason for the extra catcher is simple: the backstop hadn't been invented yet!

The Equipment, Early On

And then there's the equipment used in those days.

Bats

At first, huge, club-like bats were used, some with flat, paddle-shaped faces. A rule in 1859 outlawed the super-large monster bats. In response, players began using extra-*long* bats . . . which were outlawed by another rule, one enacted in 1876.

The ball

Today, a small cork ball forms the center of a baseball. Tightly wrapped layers of rubber and yarn surround the cork. Two strips of white cowhide, sewn together with thick red

Bats from the 1870's (far left) to more recent times. The third bat was Ty Cobb's; the fourth was Babe Ruth's.

thread, cover the insides of the ball. For quite some time—maybe longer than you'd guess—the cover was made of horsehide rather than cowhide. In fact, this didn't change until 1974! For this reason, baseballs today are sometimes still referred to as "horsehides."

Gloves

There were a lot of bright red, stinging hands in the early days of baseball. Not until 1875 were baseball gloves invented, and at first they were only for catchers.

1890s-style glove.

Made of leather, they were small and unpadded—but they were better than nothing. Pretty soon, the rest of the players, copying the catchers, began wearing gloves, too.

Over the years, improvements were made. Padding was added, the fingers were laced together, and a "pocket" was put in between the thumb and index finger.

Catcher's mask

Gloves protected the catchers' hands. But the ball was still smashing up their faces. Black eyes, busted noses, and broken teeth were their lot in life. But then in 1875, along came a man named Fred Thayer. In that year he invented the catcher's mask, modeling it after the masks used in fencing (sword fighting). Ten years later, chest protectors for catchers were introduced, and in 1908, the first shin guards were strapped on.

Old Umps, Old Rules

Strike four, you're out!

From the beginning days of baseball, there's always been an umpire. Then, as now, he called the shots and made sure the rules were followed—and got booed by somebody no matter what call he made. In that respect, he was in the same position, then as now. But early in the nineteenth century, there *were* differences. For one thing, back then it was customary for the umpire *to sit in a rocking chair!* The rules he enforced were different, too. Most importantly, *four* strikes, not three, was an out, and it took *nine* bad pitches ("balls") for the batter to get a "walk" to first base.

Cartwright Gets It Right!

These old rules—and the old boxlike shape of the playing field—were changed by Alexander Cartwright. Cartwright, in the opinion of many, was the real "father" of modern baseball. It was Cartwright, not Doubleday, who in 1845 laid out the diamond-shaped playing field like that of today.

In Cartwright's version of the game, there were only three bases. The batter stood in the "batting box," next to home plate, and to score, he had to run around the bases and back to where he'd started—"home." Initially, home was a heavy "plate" of iron, which is why it's still called "home plate" to this day. The pitching mound then was 45 feet from home plate; today it's 60' 6".

Next, Cartwright changed a lot of the rules. Four balls became a walk, three strikes an out. The players had to bat in turn, in a regular order. A runner was out if he interfered with a fielder or touched a ball in play. After three outs the players changed sides—from offense to defense. Finally, Cartwright came up with the idea of nine players on a team and nine "innings," a term derived from the medieval English word *innung* (meaning "to get in"). The idea behind the inning was to ensure each team would have an equal number of chances "to get in" to bat during the course of a game.

So far, so good. All of these rules were very sensible and are still with us

Cartwright's 1845 Field

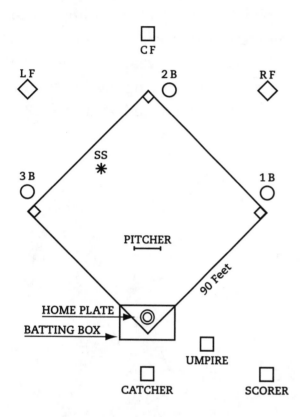

- - - - - - - - - - - - - - -
What's known as the "hot corner" in baseball?
- - - - - - - - - - - - - - -

Answer: third base

today. Cartwright did, however, come up with one rule that was *really* bad—so bad that if we'd kept it, it would have eliminated one of the most exciting aspects of the game. The rule made it almost impossible to hit a home run! The rule stated that only "one base [is] allowed when the ball is hit [out of] the field when struck."

Uniforms—Cartwright never thought of them. Up to and during his era, the players wore street shoes, wool pants, flannel shirts, and straw hats—or anything else they wanted. Not until the end of the Civil War in 1865 did the uniform come into being. First, the straw hats were discarded. Instead, players took to wearing the visored caps of Civil War soldiers, and it was from these that the modern baseball cap evolved. The cleated shoes of today were modeled after spiked shoes worn by golfers. Flannel pants and shirts were adopted during the 1870s. At first, teams wore any color uniforms they chose. The result was two teams might be wearing exactly the same color! To end the confusion, in 1882 it was decreed that pro teams had to wear only specified hues.

What two positions comprise the "battery" in modern baseball?

Baseball has gone through countless changes since the "olden days"—when players wore straw hats instead of caps, used their bare hands instead of gloves,

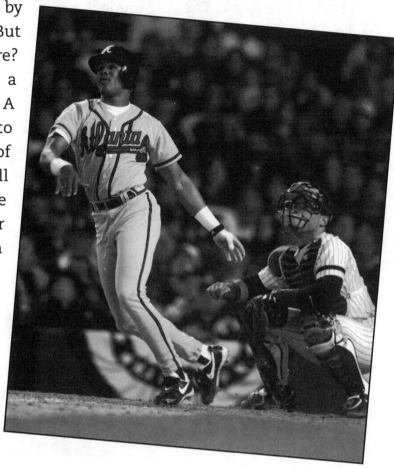

and could put out a runner by "plugging" him with the ball. But how about baseball in the future? It most likely will go through a great many more changes. A century or so from now, to future generations, the brand of baseball we play today will probably seem pretty strange and dated . . . just another phase of baseball way back in the "olden days."

Ed Delahanty hit four home runs in an 1896 game, and as a prize received

A) $4000
B) four days off
C) four boxes of chewing gum

Five

POOL
A LAWN GAME GETS TABLED

You're a kid living in England in the Middle Ages. One of your good friends invites you over to shoot a few games of pool (pocket billiards). "Love to," you say, and the two of you head on over to his place. There you play for a couple of hours or more, and have a great time. One strange thing, though: your friend doesn't have a pool table!

Time Out for an Explanation

Playing pool without a pool table sounds crazy. But during the Middle Ages, that's the way it was. Instead of a table, the game was played on the floor. The balls were large, wooden things. And they were knocked around with big wooden clubs, instead of cue sticks.

Bowling to Billiards

Going back even further, to the very beginning, billiards wasn't even an indoor game. It got its start as an outdoor form of bowling known as "lawn bowls." In this game, players rolled a large, round ball of stone at a smaller "target" ball.

Rain! In England, where lawn bowls had long been extremely popular, it rains a great deal. And cloudbursts often sent the bowlers running for cover.

They tried taking the game inside, but it didn't work out very well, not at first. It was too easy to hit the target ball in the limited playing area of a room. So instead of rolling the balls, they whacked them around with heavy wooden clubs. And instead of a target ball, a cone was set up, the object being to knock it over. To get to the cone, the ball had to be driven through a weird obstacle course of hoops, arches, and pegs. There was even one version of the game that was a miniature battle; instead of pegs and hoops, tiny forts were set up. To win, a player had to knock down his opponents' forts while protecting his own.

"Aargh, My Achin' Back!"

Bending over and whacking at a ball on the floor hurt the players' backs. And that led to the biggest change of all in the game: the action was moved up onto a table. The pool table was born!

Setting the Table

To keep the ball from rolling off the table, wooden bumpers were nailed around the edges. Next, rubber strips, or "cushions," were added, which gave the ball more bounce and protected the table. Finally, the table was covered with felt, which made for a truer shot. The felt—at least at first—was always green, and you can probably guess why. Green symbolized the fact the game had first been played on grass.

After a while, players started getting bored with hitting the ball at a cone. They wanted something more challenging, something that required more skill. Someone came up with the idea of cutting round holes into the sides of the table. So the ball wouldn't fall through the holes to the floor, pocket-like bags were attached for the balls to plop into. From then on the goal of the game became to sink a ball into a pocket rather than to topple the cone. Originally there were only two pockets, one at each end of the table. Later this was changed to four, with a pocket in each corner. Finally, side pockets were added, creating the six-pocket table of today.

On Cue

When the action moved from the floor to the table, the big, clunky club became a problem. For a time, players tried turning the club around. They held the big, fat end and pushed the ball with the smaller, narrower end. But this was still pretty awkward.

Methinks a more dainty device is needed, Lord Frumpberger.

Players realized a more delicate instrument was needed. Eventually, a long, slender stick of wood was found to do the trick. The French called it a *cue*, which means "tail," and this word remains with us today.

On the Ball

Over the years, the ball has been changing right along with everything else. Stone balls were used on the grass. For the indoor bowling-on-the-floor game, wooden balls were used, then balls of super-hard rubber. The first ones used on a table were made of brass. Then someone thought of ivory. But elephants didn't think much of the idea of having their tusks turned into pool balls, and neither did people who liked elephants. In the early 1970s, ivory was outlawed, and today billiard balls are made of an ivory-like synthetic.

Pool Gets Popular

Until the seventeenth century, only a very few people knew of billiards. Then, toward the end of that century, King Louis XIV of France made the sport popular almost overnight. The king had a habit of eating too much, too fast, and as a result often suffered from indigestion. The royal physician suggested mild exercise after meals. The king tried billiards. Not only did this

relieve the royal tummy, but King Louis loved the game. He quickly became an ardent player, and following his example, people all over Europe started taking up the sport.

One Game, Two Names

Why does the sport have two names? At first it had only one name, billiards, which comes from the French word *billiart*, meaning a "stick." Then as now, billiards was often a betting game in which players competed for all the money thrown into a pot. The French had a slang term for money wagered in this way. They called it the *poule*, meaning "hen," which is why the game today is often called pool.

> What's a "century" in billiards?

Billiards and the Bizarre

Like all sports, pool has had some pretty odd moments. In the 1790s, a French prisoner asked to stay in jail longer. The reason? The jail was the only place in town that had a pool table! Louis Fox of the U.S. also took the game seriously—a little too seriously. During a title match in the U.S. in 1865, a fly landed on the cue ball just as he took a shot. Because of the distraction, he missed the shot and lost the match. Fox killed the fly . . . then went and killed himself. Last but not least, we come to Henry Lewis. Henry had kind of a strange way of playing pool. In 1922, he had a run of forty-six . . . knocking the balls in one after the other, using his nose instead of a cue stick!

Six

GOLF
"LINKS" TO THE PAST

- -

The Roamin' Romans

Chariot races. Fights to the death. Feeding Christians to the lions. The ancient Romans did all those things. In between, they played golf.

Pagnacia—that's what they called their brand of golf. Both men and women played. In their togas and sandals, they set up targets—arrangements of sticks and small blocks of wood on the ground. Then, using a bent stick, the players took turns whacking a ball of stone or hardened leather at the targets, trying to knock them over.

Conquering other countries was always a high-priority activity for the Romans. But even soldiers need time out for fun and games. When they went tramping off to war, they took their *pagnacia* equipment with them.

Dutch Treat

After going from place to place, pillaging, plundering, and slaughtering, the Romans taught the survivors *pagnacia*. The Dutch, in particular, took a drubbing by the Romans during the first century A.D. At the same time, they really took to *pagnacia*. They improved it, changed it, and even gave it its present name. The word "golf" comes from the Dutch word *kolf*, meaning "club."

Instead of out on the grass, the Dutch usually played in a paved courtyard called a *Kolf Bann*. The players tried to hit, with as few strokes as possible, two sticks placed at opposite ends of the court. The ball was a big thing. Made of wood, it was the size of a grapefruit and weighed two pounds!

Even the cold winters in Holland didn't stop the Dutch from playing golf. They strapped on their skates, grabbed up their *kolf* clubs, and played on the ice!

Scotland: A "Hole" New Game

From Holland, golf spread to Scotland. And that's where it really turned into the game we know today. The Scots played in open fields, and the object was to knock a small ball into a hole in the ground instead of at a target.

At first, like the Dutch, the Scots used tree branches with curved ends as clubs. Then they started using their brains. The Scots were the ones who came up with the idea of attaching separate heads of wood, stone, or metal to thin shafts. The heads were bound to the shafts with wet leather which shrank as it dried, creating a tight, secure bond.

A Worldwide Hit

By the early nineteenth century, golf was taking off around the world. Wanting to make a buck, sporting goods manufacturers entered the picture and began coming out with all sorts of new equipment.

The Club

At first, most clubs looked like the putters of today. Then came "drivers" for long shots, and "spoons" and "baffies," which had scoop-like heads for hitting lofty, looping shots.

The Scots preferred hickory shafts with metal heads. Manufacturers made plenty of these; at the same time, they experimented with all sorts of other materials. Though a little heavy, solid

> *What golf club is used to hit the first shot on a long hole?*

iron clubs worked pretty well. Steel worked about as well as iron, or better. Bamboo was given a shot, but totally flopped.

In the 1920s, Americans invented clubs with tubular steel shafts. At first they were outlawed. Why? Because they worked too well! Such clubs greatly increased the distance a ball could be hit—and that created a problem: it meant golf courses would have to be made bigger. Not until 1926 was the new tubular steel shaft officially accepted, and the courses, as predicted, got larger.

The Bag

In the early days of golf, the clubs were just carried loosely under the arm. But then, in England in the 1870s, a retired sailmaker came up with the idea of the golf bag. Stitching canvas and strips of leather together, the elderly man, who worked part-time at a golf course, made the first bag as a gift for a friend.

Answer: driver

The Ball

The golf ball. It's probably gone through more changes than any other piece of sports equipment. The first ones were round stones, followed by balls of hardened leather or solid wood.

Then along came the "featherie." The featherie consisted of a little leather cover stuffed with boiled goose feathers and sewn together. To make it hard, a volume of goose feathers which would fill a bucket was shoved into the tiny cover!

Though probably not as bird brained an invention as it sounds, the featherie had flaws. Quite a few, in fact. Making them was a long, slow process, which made them expensive. And since they were little brown things, they easily got lost out on the course. This particular problem was at least partly solved by painting them white. But the featherie had other shortcomings that weren't so easily fixed. Repeated whacking eventually knocked it out of shape, and if hit especially hard, the thing would burst open . . . and instead of a ball, nothing but feathers would go flying! And maybe even most annoying of all to golfers, a featherie simply would not travel very far. Whacking a Wiffle Ball—that's more or less what hitting a featherie was like.

In 1848, a ball was invented that was made of solid gutta-percha, a very hard type of rubber. After a while it was found that an old, nicked-up ball flew farther and straighter than a new, smooth one. Instead of waiting for balls to get battered up, golfers began cutting little nicks all over them. In time, golf ball manufacturers began molding balls with patterns of little dimples. These solid rubber balls, which were known as "gutties," were in use for over half a century. Then, around 1900, rubber-core balls like those we use today were invented by Americans.

What did Floyd Rood "drive" across the US?

The Tee

A *tuitse* is what the Dutch called it. A *tuitse* was a small, cone-shaped mound of sand from which Dutch golfers hit balls. Over the centuries, the *tuitse* became the tee, a little wooden peg with a cuplike top in which to set the ball before hitting it.

The Cup

In the early days of golf, the holes had no standard size. Their present diameter came about totally by chance. One day a pair of Scottish golfers found that one of the holes on the course where they were playing was badly misshapen and caving in. Looking around for something with which to repair it, they spotted a short section of drainpipe. They inserted it into the hole—and just like that, created the first "cup." Because it happened to measure 4½ inches across, all cups are now that size.

The Course

The first golf courses were just grass-covered meadows. The number of holes depended upon the amount of good land available. Sometimes the golfers played two or three holes. Sometimes they played thirty or forty!

Eighteen-hole courses became the fashion in 1764. In that year, it was decided that a golf course should be nine holes—played "out and back." Later, instead of playing the same nine holes twice, nine more holes were added, which made the eighteen-hole course we still use today.

Golfing Goofs

In golf, as in all sports, knowing the rules is pretty important. Not knowing them can be—and often has been—the difference between winning and losing. In a 1985 tournament, T.C. Chen hit his ball into the air— then hit it again. On the sixteenth hole of the 1950 U.S. Open, Lloyd Mangrum picked up his ball and blew a gnat off it before putting it down again and chipping onto the putting green. And in the 1983 Canadian Open, Andy Bean (showing off a little) tapped the ball into the cup with the *grip* of his putter instead of the head.

Bean should have used his head. The rules say the head is the only part of the club with which the ball can be hit. They also say you can't pick a ball up during the course of play unless it's on the putting green. And of course, you can't hit a ball twice on the same swing. For their golfing goof-ups, Bean, Mangrum, and Chen all received penalty strokes—which in each case caused them to lose a match they might otherwise have won.

Last, but not least, we have Colleen Walker—and her scorecard problem. Golfers, by rule, have to keep their own scores. Costing her over $20,000 and more than one tournament during the 1980s, Ms. Walker kept getting mixed up and signing someone else's scorecard—an automatic disqualification. Poor Ms. Walker: she was great with her woods, irons, and putters, but not very sharp with a pencil!

Seven

BASKETBALL
HOW IT ALMOST BECAME BOXBALL

Hoops, Aztec-Style

In the sixteenth century, the Aztecs of Mexico played a very odd, super-nasty brand of basketball. Called *ollamalitzli*, the object of the game was to put a solid rubber ball through a stone ring placed high at one end of the court. Kicking, gouging, tripping, hair-pulling, punching—everything was legal. Scoring one point won the game. Members of the winning team were really happy. Their reward was to go and take the clothes and jewelry right off the spectators as they stood there! The captain of the defeated team got the worst end of the deal: for being the leader of the losers, his head was chopped off!

Naismith Nails It

Only recently have archaeologists learned about *ollamalitzli*. The inventor of modern basketball, Dr. James Naismith, had never heard of the game. Here's what happened. . . .

James Naismith was the youngest and newest physical education teacher at the International YMCA Training School (now Springfield College) in Springfield, Massachusetts. One freezing December morning in 1891, he trudged across campus through the snow and then down to the school's basement gymnasium. There he found two other P.E. teachers grumbling and grousing. The school's president had told them to come up with a new sport that students could play indoors on cold winter days. But so far they hadn't come up with a single decent idea.

After the other two P.E. teachers gave up and left, Naismith looked around the empty gym, trying to think of a game that could be played there. His first idea was to set up goal posts at both ends of the gym. Using a rugby ball, the kids could play sort of an indoor-type football. *Nah,* he thought. *It'd be too rough, and there'd be too many broken bones when the kids crash into the hardwood floor.*

Discarding the scheme, Naismith came up with the idea of "boxball." Two wooden boxes would be nailed to either end of the gym, and the kids would play by tossing a football to teammates who would then try to get the ball in the box.

One problem: when Naismith asked the janitor for wooden boxes, there weren't any around. "But I *do* have a couple of peach baskets in the storage room," the janitor said.

Making do, Naismith nailed the baskets to the wall. First he placed them at six feet. Realizing this would make it too easy to score, he raised the baskets to ten feet—the same height as today. Naismith took a few practice shots using a football, but the egg-shaped ball bounced around too crazily to go in. Naismith noticed a soccer ball laying in a corner. He gave it a shot—and scored the first "basket" ever!

9 to 5

The next day, the kids in Naismith's first P.E. class played the game—and loved it. Since there were eighteen kids in the class, he put nine players on each team. For years, the specified number for a team was nine.

The first basketball team, with James Naismith (wearing suit)

Later, this was reduced to seven, then it jumped back up to eight, then went down to five, as today.

True or False?

James Naismith invented the football helmet.

Shoots & Ladders

The peach baskets weren't too sturdy. They kept getting smashed up, and soon metal trash cans were used instead. Then came metal rims with net-like bags of heavy cord.

Incredibly, during the first decade of the game, no one thought of the open-ended basket. A successful shot was one in which the ball ended up caught inside the basket—either in the peach basket, trash can, or net bag. Each time a score was made, somebody had to climb up a ladder and get the ball out!

Getting the ball out got to be pretty annoying. Obviously, a change was needed. But instead of just cutting the bottom out of the thing, equipment manufacturers went off on a weird tangent. They started competing with each other,

Answer: true

making basketball baskets that had pull-down chains. The chain temporarily opened the bottom of the basket, releasing the ball.

Finally, in 1896, someone finally hit on the obvious. No one knows the man's name. All that's known about him is that he played for a semipro team—and that one day he got a pair of scissors and cut the bottom out of the net basket. At last, the days of ladder-climbing were over!

Behind the Backboard

However, there was another problem to be dealt with. At times, in the early days of the game, overenthusiastic fans tried to do their bit to help their team win. Taking a seat in the balcony as close to the basket as possible, they used their hands, sticks, or even umbrellas to knock opponents' shots away from the basket and push in those by their own team.

To put a stop to this interference, backboards were introduced. At first they were made of wire mesh. But that didn't work so well; fans still managed to get objects through the meshing. The wire mesh was replaced with plain wood. Finally, along came glass, so spectators behind the backboards could see the action.

Dribble Ball

Imagine what a mess basketball would be if the players could run with the ball! Early on, Naismith realized that this would ruin the game, and declared that "running with the ball in one's hands is to be strictly prohibited." Instead, the ball could be advanced by passing it. However, before passing it, a player could bounce the ball as many times as he or she wanted. Players soon started taking advantage of this loophole in the rules, running as they bounced the ball. The "dribble" had begun!

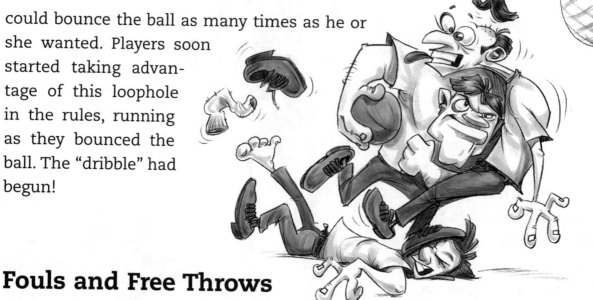

Fouls and Free Throws

Another of Naismith's original basketball rules was that the ball couldn't be "kicked or smashed with the fist." Also, "there was to be no tackling, tripping, slapping, or knocking down of other players." Penalties were called for these—and other—violations.

At first, there were no free throws for fouling. Instead, three fouls in a row by a team resulted in the other team being given one point. The fouls had to be consecutive—with no fouls being committed in the meantime by the opposing team.

The idea of free throws came into being in 1893. But the free throw was not shot by the person who was fouled! Instead, each team had its own "specialist" free-throw shooter. The specialist free-throwers were done away with in 1923, so that a player had to make his own free-throw shot when fouled.

Making a Point

> *What basketball shot was once illegal?*

Originally, a free throw was worth three points, and so were *all* shots made when the ball was in play. In 1896, free throws were reduced from three points to one point, and field goals were reduced from three points to two. Many years later, the three-point basket made a comeback—but only for extra-long shots.

Answer: the slam dunk

Much too Jumpy

Wilt Chamberlain holds the NBA record for most points scored in a single basketball game. How many points did he score?

A) 51   B) 84   C) 100

For nearly half a century, there was always a "center jump" after each score. To say the least, this totally slowed down the action. Not until 1938 was the center jump eliminated, and the ball was put back into play by the team scored upon.

Ties and Tie-Breakers

Today when time is up and the game is tied, the teams play as many five-minute overtimes as necessary until one team wins. In his original rules, Naismith wrote: "In case of a draw the game may, by agreement of the captains, either be considered to be concluded or may be continued until *one* goal is made."

The One and Only

The history of basketball is unlike that of any sport. Sure, there have been all kinds of changes in the rules, equipment, and techniques of play. That's just natural. The amazing thing is that this sport was the brainstorm of *one* person. James Naismith, pure and simple, invented the game. Of the thirteen original rules he wrote down one cold day in 1891, twelve are still in effect.

James Naismith went on to become an ordained Presbyterian minister and a medical doctor. Until his death at the ripe old age of 88, he remained a sports enthusiast and physical fitness nut—and had the pleasure of seeing his brainstorm become one of the most popular games in the U.S.

James Naismith

Answer: C) 100

Eight

BADMINTON
THE SPORT OF FORTUNE-TELLERS

- -

A Backward Look Forward

Babylonia was an ancient civilization near where Iran and Iraq are today. It was kind of a strange place to live. For one thing, fortune-telling was a really big deal there. Almost all the ancient Babylonians would go to a priest who, for a fee, would tell them what the future had in store.

The priest had a whole bag of tricks—lots of different ways to tell your future. Sometimes he'd toss dice or

What'll it be? Dice? Dreams? Or a look-see at my sheep's liver?

bones, and as he looked over their arrangement on the ground, he'd tell you if good things or bad were coming your way. Other times he'd ask you to tell him your dreams, and he'd interpret them. Then there was the gross sheep liver bit. Sometimes he'd take a sheep's liver, cut it up, and looking around in the mess, fill you in on the future he foresaw for you.

Badminton, Babylonian-Style

Another fortune-telling technique (though the priests didn't foresee it) would, centuries later, turn into the game of badminton. The whole thing was a ceremony. And it went something like this. . . .

A crowd gathered. Incense was lit, and the aroma filled the air. Drums were banged. Magical chants were sung. And then out came a priest followed by two people, each holding a wooden paddle. The priest called for silence. A hush fell over the crowd. Then the two people with the paddles batted a ball of tightly wound wool yarn back and forth. The length of time they could keep the ball in play supposedly revealed how long they would live.

Gradually, the ceremony took on a slightly different meaning. Since the two people intentionally kept the woolen ball in play as long as possible, they were not only finding out about their future, they were also influencing it. That is, since they had a degree of control over the outcome of the ball-batting, they had a degree of control over their life spans.

I'm only going to live to be 7 years old! Sniffle. Snort. Sob.

Since you're already 15, Ninazu, I wouldn't worry too much.

The Game Gets Going

Over the centuries, the fortune-telling hocus-pocus was forgotten and people just batted the ball back and forth for sport—just for the fun of it. From Babylonia, the sport spread to many different places. One of these was Poona, India. Because it was so popular in this town, the game came to be known as *Poona*.

In the sixteenth century, English sailors, merchants, and explorers visited India. There they learned the game and brought it home with them. Soon, the English replaced the wooden paddle with a racket. At first the racket was a wooden frame with a leather center. Later, it had leather strings stretched over the frame. Also, instead of a woolen ball, the English used a piece of cork into which feathers had been stuck. At first, the feathers stuck straight out. Players soon found, however, that a fan-shaped arrangement of feathers made for a truer, more "bird-like" flight.

Shuttlecock Day

Because they went back and forth (shuttled), and were partly made of rooster or "cock" feathers, the missiles—and the game—were renamed "shuttlecocks." Kids especially enjoyed the game, particularly on Shrove Tuesday, a Christian holiday in which being happy and having fun were the order of the day. The sport became so popular that in some English towns the day came to be known as "Shuttlecock Day." The streets were crowded with people of all ages batting their feathered corks back and forth through the air.

A Bash at Badminton House

In the nineteenth century, there was an Englishman named the Duke of Beaufort. The duke was a real sports lover, and he especially liked shuttlecocks. One weekend in 1870, he had a shuttlecocks party at his home, a mansion called Badminton House. Everybody played—men, women, kids. The party was a smashing success, so much so that the game's popularity, which had been decreasing a bit, suddenly skyrocketed in England. In fact, because of the party, the game took on a new name—badminton, the name of the place where the party had been held.

Marching to America

Americans did not take to the sport until the end of World War I in 1918. At that time, American soldiers were returning from Europe. Some had been in England, where they had learned badminton. Bringing rackets and shuttlecocks—and their enthusiasm for the game—home with them, they launched a new sports craze in the U.S.

Badminton today

(Sir) Thomas Cup

By 1939, badminton had become popular worldwide, and a man by the name of Sir George Thomas decided it was time for international competition. For the winning country, naturally, there would have to be a special trophy, as in other sports. Because of World War II, Sir Thomas's dream was put on hold until 1948, when the first world championship matches were held. The winning team was from Malaya. Beating Denmark 8 to 1 in the finals, the Malayans captured the first world title and walked off with the trophy—which, appropriately, is called the Thomas Cup.

The Duke of Beaufort, after whose home badminton is named, wrote The Badminton Library, *a 28-volume encyclopedia on sports origins, records, and rules of play. Strangely, the duke described and discussed every sport except one—badminton!*

Nine

BOXING

ALL A BOUT IT

- -

It's mankind's oldest and bloodiest sport. Boxing. It's been around since the beginning, ever since man learned to make a fist.

Boxing in Baghdad

Go back seven thousand years. You're in Baghdad, a city in the Middle East. The houses are made of mud-brick. The streets are unpaved. It's nighttime, but there are no streetlights—just torches to light the way. From an alley comes noise and commotion. And there, in the flickering torchlight, a crowd is yelling as two men punch and pound each other with their bare fists. Finally, there's a roar from the crowd. One of the men goes down in a bloody heap—dead.

The other, though battered and bruised, is congratulated and his hand is raised in victory. Bets are paid off with gold and silver coins. Those who bet on the winner are smiling. Frowning and grumbling, their pockets empty, those who bet on the dead guy wander off into the dark of the city.

The next day, one of the spectators has an inspiration. Using a crude hammer and chisel, he scratches a picture into a stone tablet. The picture shows the action of the night before.

Centuries pass. The tablet just lays there, half-buried. Then one day in 1927, an archaeologist, Dr. E. A. Speiser, finds it. Though badly faded and weathered by the passage of time, it is still quite clear what the etching depicts: two men squaring off for a prize fight.

Beyond Baghdad

Several such tablets have been found in and around Baghdad. At least seven thousand years old, they're the earliest recordings we have of boxing. But the sport is probably even older. It was popular in many places other than the Middle East, too. For example, long ago in India men fought with their hands wrapped in layers of string. On the Tonga Islands, boxing matches were held as regular performances on command of the king. On the Mortlocks, another island group in the Pacific, the boxers turned their fists into deadly weapons. They armed them with rows of shark teeth!

Greco-Roman Rough Stuff

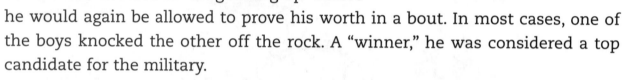

Boxing was used by the Greeks to prepare boys to become soldiers. In training bouts, two boys sat on flat rocks facing each other. Bare-fisted, they began slugging it out. If one of the boys got up and ran away, he was branded a coward and in need of "toughening up" before he would again be allowed to prove his worth in a bout. In most cases, one of the boys knocked the other off the rock. A "winner," he was considered a top candidate for the military.

Athletic contests for adult Greek men were even rougher. The sport had no ring, rules, or rounds. Two men bashed and battered each other ruthlessly while moving over a wide area. A fight ended only when one of the boxers lay beaten and bleeding, no matter how long this took.

Boxing matches were a popular feature of Greek festivals and holidays. Oddly, they were also sometimes held at *funerals*! It was believed that the person about to be buried would enjoy the contest so much that he would not want to turn into a ghost and come back to haunt the living!

Around 500 B.C. the Greeks added a new element to the sport. Fighters wound soft strips of leather around their hands and arms. These protected the knuckles and added to the force of the blow. Then gloves replaced the strips. Made of hardened leather, the gloves had cutting edges and were fearsome weapons.

Around 300 B.C. there was another development in the sport. A circle was drawn in the dirt, and the combatants were not allowed to move out of the prescribed area. This was the beginning of the boxing "ring."

When the Romans conquered Greece around 150 B.C., they enslaved hundreds of the conquered Greek soldiers. In Rome, the captured Greeks were used in gladiatorial contests, including an especially violent and bloody type of boxing. For these contests, the Romans invented the *cestus*, a leather hand-covering that was weighted with pieces of iron and had metal studs and spikes fixed over the knuckles. The gladiators fought to the death, with the only reward for the winner being to live to fight again another day.

In Rome, boxing turned into something far too low to be called a sport. It was so bloody and murderous that people no longer wanted to see it. Eventually use of the *cestus* was banned, and during the latter half of the first century B.C., boxing in any form was outlawed.

In 1952, how many boxers died from injuries suffered in the ring?

A) none
B) three
C) seventeen

England: Boxing's Re-Creation

For hundreds of years the sport almost completely vanished. It did not make a comeback until the seventeenth century in England, at which time and place it got its modern name. Funnily enough, the word "boxing" came into being as a joke, as a playful use of language. In seventeenth-century England, the word "box" was a synonym for the word "gift." When fighters battled, they exchanged "boxes." The boxes, though, were not gifts of love—they were punches thrown into each other's bodies and faces!

Soon, boxing matches again became savage, super-bloody spectacles. Men fought bare-knuckled and often wore shoes with spikes or studs. Not only did the boxers bash each other with their fists, they kicked and stomped each other with their deadly footwear. Eye-gouging, head-butting, wrestling, and body-slamming were also part of the action. Both the winner and loser usually ended up a bloody mess.

Broughton: Square Rings and Fair Fights

In 1743, a boxing promoter named Jack Broughton did a lot to get the action under control and make boxing far less gory. At the London arena where he staged matches, Broughton outlawed wrestling, kicking, and gouging, and set down the rule "that you cannot hit a man when he is down." Also, if a boxer fell and was not able to get up within thirty seconds, he was declared "knocked out of time," and the match was over.

Broughton was responsible for other important changes as well. A big problem in those days was that fans would sometimes get so excited they'd jump into the ring and enter into the fighting—and beat up the boxers, the trainers, the ref, and even each other! To prevent these wild free-for-alls, Broughton made the ring square, enclosed it with ropes, and raised it six feet off the ground—where it remains today.

Along with everything else he did for the sport, Broughton also invented the modern boxing glove. However, back then it was worn only for sparring and training.

Queensberry: Rounds, Rules, and Gloves

The marquess of Queensberry, another Englishman, was responsible for getting gloves on the hands of boxers in public bouts, and otherwise making the sport more civilized. In 1867, he laid down the basic rules of boxing that we follow today. The rules said the fighters would wear padded gloves, the ring would be canvas, and there would be three-minute rounds with one-minute rest periods in between.

A Round and A Round We Go . . . Where We Stop, Nobody Knows!

Though he came up with the idea of "rounds" in boxing matches, Queensberry never said anything about *how many* there would be. Fights lasted as many rounds as necessary until somebody got decked.

In 1892, Harry Sharpe knocked out Frank Crosby in *seventy-seven* rounds. In 1890, Danny Needham and Pat Kerrigan fought to a draw in *one hundred* rounds. But the longest fight ever was an 1893 match between Andy Bowen and Jack Burke, which lasted for over seven hours and went on for 110 rounds! The referee declared the bout "no contest" when both men were too tired and smashed-up to continue. Not until the early twentieth century were fights limited to definite numbers of rounds—putting an end to "endless" fights.

> *True or False?*
> In 1892, a woman by the name of Hessie Donahue fought John L. Sullivan and knocked him to the canvas.

Short Stuff

The Bowen-Burke bout was the longest fight on record. The shortest ever was a 1946 contest between Al Couture and Ralph Walton. When the starting bell sounded, Couture shot across the ring at Walton. Walton, still in the process of adjusting his mouthpiece, was knocked cold *one-half second* after the fight started!

Offbeat Bouts

The shortest-ever and longest-ever fights were pretty strange affairs. But what was the most bizarre, totally strangest fight of all time? Some would say it was the 1997 bout in which Mike Tyson bit off part of Evander Holyfield's right ear. Or maybe it was a 1978 fight in which Sugar Ray Leonard knocked out Tom Kelly . . . the *referee!* But then there's the 1959 match between Henry Wallitsch and Bartolo Soni. As far as bizarreness goes, this one probably tops the list.

Here's what happened. For the whole fight, Soni kept running and dancing around the ring with Wallitsch lumbering after him. Wallitsch hadn't landed a single punch, and he was getting extremely angry and frustrated. Finally, in the third round, Wallitsch got Soni in a clinch and saw his big chance. Wallitsch wound up, and with every ounce of strength he could muster, threw a mighty punch . . . and missed everything. The force of the swing carried him across the ring and over the ropes. Taking one right on the chin (from the arena floor) he landed a place in sports history . . . as the only boxer ever to knock *himself* out!

Read all about it! Wallitsch KOs Wallitsch in the third!

DAILY BLAB

KNOCKOUT?

More Fun Reading From Simon & Schuster

THE ULTIMATE ASTEROID BOOK:
The Inside Story on the Threat from the Skies
by Mary Barnes

Everything you've ever wanted to know about
the real-life space invaders featured in your
favorite science fiction movies.

BUNNICULA'S WICKEDLY WACKY WORD GAMES:
A Book for Word Lovers & Their Pencils!
by James Howe, illustrated by Alan Daniel

Sixteen terrific activities, including word searches,
tips for writing scary stories, and much more.

BUNNICULA'S PLEASANTLY PERPLEXING PUZZLERS:
A Book of Puzzles, Mazes, & Whatzits!
by James Howe, illustrated by Alan Daniel

Magical mazes, crazy crossword puzzles, and
boggling brain benders.

THE ULTIMATE RUGRATS FAN BOOK
by Jefferson Graham

An up-close look at the hit show, including
a complete episode guide, trivia, photos, and more.